This book belongs to:

....

....

....

Retold by Gaby Goldsack
Illustrated by Ruth Galloway (Advocate)
Designed by Blue Sunflower Creative

Language consultant: Betty Root

ISBN 1-84461-212-0

Marks and Spencer p.l.c.
PO Box 3339
Chester, CH99 9QS
www.marksandspencer.com

Snow White
and the
Seven Dwarfs

Helping your Child to Read

Learning to read is an exciting challenge for most children. From a very early age, sharing story books with children, talking about the pictures and guessing what might happen next are all very important parts of the reading experience.

Sharing reading

Set aside a regular quiet time to share reading with younger children, or to be on hand to encourage older children as they develop into independent readers.

First Readers are intended to encourage and support the early stages of learning to read. They present well-loved tales that children will happily listen to again and again. Familiarity helps children to identify some of the words and phrases.

When you feel your child is ready to move on a little, encourage them to join in so that you read the story aloud together. Always pause to talk about the pictures. The easy-to-read speech bubbles in **First Readers** provide an excellent 'joining-in' activity. The bright, clear illustrations and matching text will help children to understand the story.

Building confidence

In time, children will want to read *to* you. When this happens, be patient and give continual praise. They may not read all the words correctly, but children's substitutions are often very good guesses.

The repetition in each book is particularly helpful for building confidence. If your child cannot read a particular word, go back to the beginning of the sentence and read it together so the meaning is not lost. Most importantly, do not continue if your child is tired or simply in need of a change.

Reading aloud

The next step is to ask your child to read aloud to you. This does require patience and perseverance. Remember to give lots of encouragement and praise.

Together with other simple stories, **First Readers** will ensure that children will find reading an enjoyable and rewarding experience.

Once upon a time there was a king and a queen. They had a beautiful baby girl.

The king and queen called her Snow White.

The queen died soon after Snow White was born.

The king was sad and lonely.

But, one year later, the king married again.

The new queen was very beautiful.
She liked to look at herself in a mirror.

The queen had one special mirror. It was magic. Everyday she looked into the magic mirror and said,

"Mirror, mirror on the wall,
who is the fairest of them all?"

And the mirror would answer,

"You are the fairest."

Who is the fairest?

One day, the queen looked into the mirror and said,

"Mirror, mirror on the wall,
who is the fairest of them all?"

And the mirror said,

"You were the fairest, shining bright.
But now the fairest is Snow White."

The queen was very cross.
She called for a servant.

"Take Snow White into
the forest and kill her,"
said the queen.

The servant took Snow White into the forest.

"I don't want to kill you, run away please," he said. And he walked away.

"Please don't leave me," said Snow White. He left her near a cottage.

Snow White walked to the cottage.

She knocked at the door. There was no answer so she went in.

She saw seven little chairs around a little table. Then she saw seven little beds.

Snow White was very tired. She lay down on one of the beds.

Seven little dwarfs lived
in the cottage.

Each day they went into
the hills to dig for gold.

That night, they came back to the cottage.
They found Snow White fast asleep.
When she woke up she told them
her story.

"You can stay with us," said the dwarfs.

The next day the seven dwarfs went into the hills to dig for gold.

Snow White stayed at the cottage.

"Do not let anyone in," the dwarfs said to Snow White.

Back at the palace, the queen looked
into her magic mirror and said,

"Mirror, mirror on the wall,
who is the fairest one of all?"

And the mirror said,

"You were the fairest, shining bright.
But now the fairest is Snow White."

The queen was very cross. She put some poison in an apple. She dressed up as an old woman and went to the cottage.

Snow White opened the door and saw the old woman.

"Would you like an apple?" the old woman asked.

"Yes please," said Snow White. She took one bite and fell to the ground.

When the seven dwarfs came home, they could not wake Snow White. They were very sad.

We are very sad.

The dwarfs put Snow White in a glass box.

A prince came riding by. He saw Snow White.

"What a beautiful girl," he said.

The prince opened the glass box.
He kissed Snow White.

The kiss woke her up. She saw the
prince and fell in love with him.

"Will you marry me?" asked the prince.

"Yes!" said Snow White.

One day the queen
looked in her magic mirror
and the mirror said,

"You were the fairest,
shining bright.
But now much fairer is
Snow White."

The queen was so cross that she
disappeared.

Snow White and the prince married and
lived happily ever after.

Read and Say

How many of these words can you say? The pictures will help you. Look back in your book and see if you can find the words in the story.

queen

king

Snow White

mirror

forest

prince

cottage

bed

dwarfs

apple

Titles in this series,
subject to availability:

Beauty and the Beast
Chicken-Licken
Cinderella
The Elves and the Shoemaker
The Emperor's New Clothes
The Enormous Turnip
The Gingerbread Man
Goldilocks and the Three Bears
Hansel and Gretel
Jack and the Beanstalk
Joseph's Coat of Many Colours
Little Red Riding Hood
Noah's Ark and other Bible Stories
Rapunzel
Rumpelstiltskin
Sleeping Beauty
Snow White and the Seven Dwarfs
The Three Billy Goats Gruff
The Three Little Pigs
The Ugly Duckling